D0459082

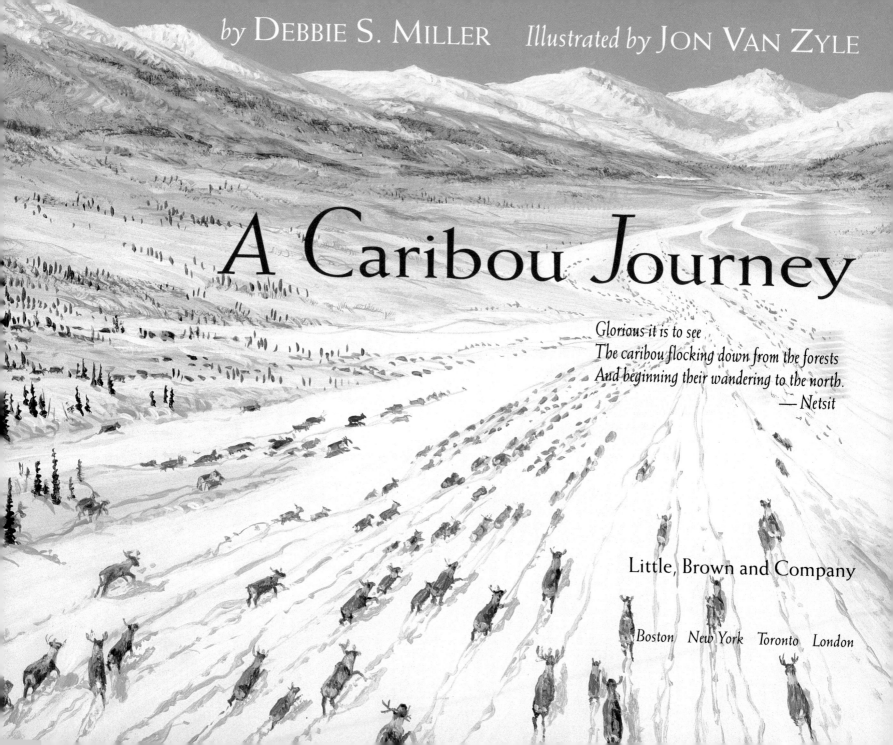

by DEBBIE S. MILLER   Illustrated by JON VAN ZYLE

A Caribou Journey

Glorious it is to see
The caribou flocking down from the forests
And beginning their wandering to the north.
— Netsit

Little, Brown and Company

Boston   New York   Toronto   London

A COLD ARCTIC WIND blows across the snow-covered mountains of northern Alaska. It is springtime, but a vast quilt of snow still covers this frozen land near the top of the world.

On a windswept ridge, a small group of caribou plods through the crusted snow. One caribou mother digs a small crater with her broad, sharp-edged hooves. She smells lichens beneath the snow. Her calf paws through the snow next to her. The young bull has learned to dig for his food by watching his mother. Soon they are rubbing their muzzles against the frozen tundra, eating mouthfuls of yellow and gray lichens.

The name *caribou* comes from the Micmac Indian word *ĝalipu* (GHAH-lee-boo), meaning "snow shoveler." Indeed, barren-ground caribou spend eight months of the year pawing through snow for lichens. They would not survive the arctic winter without these small, spongy plants. Wandering in search of food, these caribou travel farther than any other land mammal — almost three thousand miles each year.

Barren-ground caribou are the deer of the Far North. In Alaska and Canada, many herds are found scattered across the open tundra above the Arctic Circle. They are well suited for the arctic environment. The hollow, thick hairs of their tawny brown-and-white coats insulate them from the extreme cold. The pads of their hooves are covered with long hairs during the winter, and fatty tissues inside the hoof work like "antifreeze" for the caribou. Above their hooves, caribou have two long toes, called dewclaws. These give the animals extra support, like snowshoes, when they are walking through soft snow.

In the evening, the caribou rest in the middle of a frozen, snow-covered lake. The lake is a good place to rest because the caribou can watch for predators. In the spruce forest, a pack of wolves could ambush them.

Tucking his legs beneath him, the young bull lies down near his mother. While he rests, a bright full moon rises silently above the mountains. His mother's moonlit breath steams into the frigid air. As the temperature drops to thirty below zero, the lake ice cracks, sending eerie high-pitched sounds into the night.

At dawn, the hungry caribou move toward the forest to search for lichens. It is easier to dig in the woods because the forest floor is sheltered from strong winds and the snow is softer than in open areas. As they cross the lake, the mother caribou discovers a mound of lake plants known as a "push-up." A muskrat gathered the plants and pushed them up through a hole in the ice as a source of winter food.

After the mother paws the snow off the push-up, she and the young bull take a few mouthfuls of the lake plants. Beneath the ice, a muskrat inspects the food pile, then hears the crunching sound of the caribou walking on across the lake. The muskrat takes a few bites of the plants, then swims back to its den in the lake's bank.

In the forest, the mother and young bull paw and eat with the rest of the herd. Suddenly the mother stops and sniffs the air. She snorts at the young bull, warning him of danger. Then she thrusts her hind leg out to one side — an alarm signal to the other caribou. After holding this pose for a few seconds, the mother jumps onto her hind legs and bounds off. This alarm jump releases a strong scent from the glands in her hooves. Any caribou following her will smell the scent and know there is danger.

The mother runs through the forest, the young bull racing after her. Other frightened caribou bolt through the woods alongside them, panting white clouds of breath into the freezing air. Wolves are close behind.

At the edge of the forest, the mother and the young bull reach a clearing. *Crack!* Spruce branches break behind them, then a caribou groans in pain. The pack of wolves has caught one of the slower animals. The mother and young bull move on.

As spring days grow longer, the caribou feel the urge to migrate north to their summer range. They begin their long northern journey across tundra, mountains, and rivers, toward a broad plain near the Arctic Ocean. The coastal plain is the birthplace of this great herd. Many thousands of caribou will soon gather there.

The caribou walk one behind the other, following a migration route that has been used for centuries. Older cows that are familiar with the route take turns breaking trail, leading the way. As they travel north, other groups of caribou join them, like creeks flowing into a river.

Much of the snow has melted when the mother and young bull reach the treeless coastal plain. The patchy tundra is full of budding cotton grass and other plants. The caribou feast on the new growth.

The mother will soon bear another calf near the same spot where the young bull was born. After a long winter, the mother needs to gain weight and energy so she can deliver and nurse a healthy new calf.

By his first birthday, the young bull is ready to be on his own. He leaves his mother and joins other yearlings grazing on the tundra. For the first time in many months, the young bull eats without pawing through snow. He grazes until his belly is full.

In early June, the mother delivers a female calf. The twelve-pound newborn stands on her wobbly legs, nuzzling her mother. The mother licks her fur clean and becomes familiar with her scent and voice. Now the mother will be able to keep track of her among the tens of thousands of newborn calves.

Caribou produce the richest milk of all land mammals. The calf suckles several times a day and grows quickly. When the long-legged calf is just a few days old, she can run faster than a human or wolf.

The curious calf begins exploring the coastal plain. One morning, she wanders away from her mother toward a den of chattering ground squirrels. All of a sudden, the dark shadow of a golden eagle flashes across the tundra. The alarmed mother snorts, calling to her calf. Hearing the distress call, the calf runs to her mother.

Just as the golden eagle swoops down to pierce the calf with its sharp talons, the calf runs beneath her mother's belly. The mother shakes her antlers at the eagle as it dives for the calf. The eagle veers off, circles, then dives again. This time the mother rears up on her hind legs and paws at the eagle as it approaches. The eagle swerves away and flies off toward the distant mountains.

For more than two summer months in the Arctic, the sun never sets. During these endless days, thousands of caribou roam the open tundra. Calves graze alongside their mothers, who have recently shed their antlers. They share the land with many nesting birds and their chicks. The air is filled with the sounds of grunting caribou and chirping birds — and with clouds of buzzing mosquitoes.

Although the birds thrive on these insects, a caribou can lose up to one quart of blood in a week's time when the mosquitoes are at their worst. Since the caribou are shedding their winter coats, the mosquitoes can easily bite their skin. The caribou quiver and shake their bodies to get rid of them as well as other biting insects.

One afternoon, the mother and calf trot toward the Arctic Ocean with other caribou to get away from the mosquitoes. Near the ocean it is cool and breezy, and there are fewer insects. When they reach the beach, they walk into the ocean, where they find lots of floating ice. The mother and calf climb on top of a giant ice floe and lie down to rest. For a time they escape the mosquitoes.

The hot, buggy weather later drives the caribou together by the thousands. By grouping tightly together, each caribou is exposed to fewer insects. As they swarm together like bees upon a hive, the caribou feel the urge to leave the coastal plain.

Mothers, calves, yearlings, and older bulls all join together in one mass of animals. A jungle of legs moves across the tundra. The air is filled with the grunting, snorting, coughing, and bleating voices of the caribou, along with the unique clicking sound caused by tendons slipping over joints within the caribou's hooves. The calf runs to keep up with her mother. She could easily get lost in this huge crowd of more than a hundred thousand animals.

The herd crosses many creeks and rivers along its journey. The caribou's hollow hair helps them float, and their broad hooves work like paddles in the water. Caribou are strong swimmers, but some calves drown when crossing deep, swift rivers.

The calf is swimming across one such river when suddenly some rapids sweep her away from her mother. The calf paddles hard through the white water to reach land. She can barely keep her nose above the fast water. Luckily, her hooves hit a shallow section of the river. The calf scrambles out of the water onto the riverbank. She shakes the water out of her fur, then looks around for the rest of the herd. Alone and lost, the calf runs up and down the bank, bleating for her mother.

When the mother reaches the other side of the river, she finds her calf has disappeared. In the midst of thousands of caribou, she sniffs the air for the calf's scent, then trots up and down the riverbank, calling for her. Her ears flap up and down as she listens for her calf's call. With the clutter of hooves, splashing of water, and grunting of all the animals, it seems impossible that the mother will find the calf.

After several minutes, most of the herd has crossed the river and continued on across the tundra. It is then that the mother recognizes her calf bleating downstream. She runs quickly to the calf, and they are reunited. The calf suckles her mother for a few moments, then they run to catch up with the rest of the herd.

The herd continues south into the river valleys of the Brooks Range. Miles and miles of caribou trails are etched deeply into the tundra from centuries of use. In the mountains where the bright autumn colors are just beginning to show, the herd divides into smaller groups. Their southern journey takes them along winding rivers, past distant peaks and glaciers, and over rugged mountain passes.

While the mother and calf eat the last of summer's green growth, the young bull grazes with another group of yearlings, bulls, and cows in a nearby valley. He has grown a set of antlers nearly the size of his mother's, while the young calf has grown small spike antlers. Both male and female caribou grow antlers each summer — the only members of the deer family to do so. Older bulls grow the biggest antlers, which arc high above their heads.

New antlers are covered with a soft skin known as velvet. The velvet nourishes the antlers and begins to itch when the antlers are fully grown. As the mating, or rutting, season approaches, bull caribou thrash their antlers against shrubs and trees, stripping off the velvet. With polished antlers, new coats of fur, and long white manes, the handsome bulls are ready to find cows to be their mates.

The first autumn snowstorm has dusted the tundra. While the young bull playfully
butts his head with other yearlings, two of the larger bulls lower their heads and charge
each other. The yearlings move out of the way of the fighting bulls. *Crash!* The large antlers
of the two bulls clatter together. Nose to nose, they try to throw each other off balance,
digging their hooves into the ground and pushing forward with their swollen, muscular
necks. Their flared nostrils puff steam into the crisp air. Locked together, the antlers look
like tangled branches.

After several minutes of fighting, one of the bulls loses his balance, and the stronger bull rams him into a thicket of willow bushes. The defeated bull turns and runs off across the tundra, while the winner seeks the cows of his choice. In a few years, the young bull will be old enough to spar successfully for his own mates.

By October, the mountains and valleys are cloaked in snow. The caribou begin using their hooves like shovels to dig for their food. Once again, they will move all winter to find enough lichens to eat. They spread out across their vast winter range, traveling in small groups.

As night falls, the mother, calf, and young bull rest in a clearing near a dark spruce forest. As the caribou drift off to sleep, the northern lights ripple and dance across the sky. The magical curtains of shimmering light mean that winter's long, dark nights have returned. The caribou will travel many, many miles before summer comes again.

AUTHOR'S NOTE

Caribou, and their cousins the reindeer, are found in many northern regions around the world. Like the wildebeest of Africa and the buffalo that once roamed across the Great Plains, caribou often travel together in huge herds. Witnessing the migration of tens of thousands of caribou is one of the world's greatest wildlife spectacles.

Caribou have lived on the earth for countless centuries. They were hunted in prehistoric times by Cro-Magnon man in northern Europe and by the ancestors of many native peoples in North America and Asia. Today, caribou continue to be an important resource, particularly for northern indigenous people, such as the Athabaskan Indians of Alaska and Canada,

who consider caribou their source of life.

This is the story of the life cycle of caribou within the Porcupine Herd, one of the largest migratory herds in North America. Traveling thousands of miles each year, the Porcupine Herd moves back and forth between northeast Alaska and Canada's Yukon Territory. Having lived in northern Alaska, I've been fortunate enough to observe this herd over the course of many years.

Each spring the herd migrates north to the coastal plain of the Arctic National Wildlife Refuge. On this wild, open stretch of tundra the caribou give birth to tens of thousands of calves and graze freely in one of the greatest wilderness areas remaining on earth. As in many regions across the globe, resource development has been proposed on the coastal plain of the Arctic Refuge. Whether humans will have the foresight to preserve this unique wilderness area for future generations of caribou, and many other animals, is uncertain.

For Dennis,
who follows the caribou

And special thanks to Dr. David Klein,
who reviewed the manuscript and
contributed his knowledge about caribou
—D. M.

For Char,
like the caribou . . . a free spirit
—J. V. Z.

First Edition

Library of Congress Cataloging-in-Publication Data

Miller, Debbie S.
   A caribou journey / by Debbie S. Miller ; illustrated by Jon Van Zyle.
      p.   cm.
   Summary: Surveys the migrations, habits, and habitat of a herd of caribou in Alaska.
   ISBN 0-316-57380-9
   ISBN 0-316-91154-2 (UK pb)
   1. Caribou — Alaska — Juvenile literature. 2. Caribou — Alaska — Migration — Juvenile literature.   [1. Caribou.]   I. Van Zyle, Jon, ill.   II. Title.
   QL737.U55M525   1994
   599.73'57 — dc20   93-9777

SC 10 9 8 7 6 5 4 3 2 1

Published simultaneously in Canada by Little, Brown & Company (Canada) Limited and in Great Britain by Little, Brown and Company (UK) Limited

Printed in Hong Kong

The paintings in this book were done in acrylic on untempered Masonite panels. Text set in Weiss by Typographic House.